D0457550

SQUIRREL in the MUSEUM

by **Vivian Vande Velde**

illustrated by
Steve Biörkman

HOLIDAY HOUSE New York

Text copyright © 2019 by Vivian Vande Velde
Illustrations copyright © 2019 by Steve Björkman
All Rights Reserved
HOLIDAY HOUSE is registered in the U.S. Patent and Trademark Office.
Printed and bound in December 2018 at Maple Press, York, PA, USA.
First Edition
1 3 5 7 9 10 8 6 4 2
www.holidayhouse.com

Library of Congress Cataloging-in-Publication Data is available.

ISBN 978-0-8234-4167-9

To the members of my writers' groups, who keep me going:
Judy Bradbury, Alice DeLaCroix, and Marsha Hayles;

Tedd Arnold, MJ Auch, Patience Brewster,
Bruce and Kathy Coville, Cynthia DeFelice, Robin Pulver,
and Ellen Stoll Walsh;

and to Dr. Carol Johmann—honorary cousin—who
explained (patiently) how an airplane flying is science,
not magic— V. V. V.

Contents

Twitch,
the Schoolyard Squirrel

I am a very highly educated squirrel.

I always paid attention to my mother's life lessons.

Some of my mother's life lessons:

- Don't let an owl eat you.

- Don't let a weasel eat you.

- Don't let a fox eat you.

- Don't let a wolf eat you.

Because I have an inquisitive mind, I asked my mother, "What are wolves?"

She said, "I don't know. But my mother told *me* not to let wolves eat me. And her mother told her, and her mother told her, and her mother, and hers, on back as far as any squirrel could remember."

"Maybe there used to be wolves," I said, "but there aren't anymore."

"Maybe," she said. "But it would be a very bad thing for a squirrel to let a wolf eat him because his mother hadn't warned him not to."

It is always better not to get eaten.

My mother taught me other life lessons, too.

She taught me to be quick to get the food that people leave out for us, since birds think the people have put out the food for them, even though birds aren't nearly as cute as squirrels.

She taught me not to tell the birds that they aren't cute (even though it's easy to see) because it's a useful thing to get along with other animals—not counting the owls, weasels, foxes, and wolves that would eat us.

A life lesson I learned on my own, which I pass on to younger squirrels, is that while it's good to look cute, a squirrel should try not to look so cute that people try to catch you and keep you as a pet.

Besides the life lessons I learned from my mother, I

am also highly educated because I live in a schoolyard. School is where people children learn their life lessons, since—for some reason—people mothers don't teach their own young.

I like to sit on the windowsills at school and watch through the glass as the children get taught—even though a lot of the lessons they learn are not nearly as useful as the ones squirrels learn. My favorite window is by the library where my cousin, Sweetie the rat, lives in

FAMILY PHOTOS

a cage he is smart enough to get out of—but he usually chooses not to. Both of us like to listen to the library teacher read stories to the people children.

I have other cousins who live at the school. There's a hamster, and also a rabbit. Rabbits are very distant cousins to squirrels. There are also a couple of geckos who live in the science lab. I'm not at all related to them, but they are interesting, so they are honorary cousins even though it's hard to get a word in and the way they talk gives my head the wibble-wobbles.

Sometimes, one of the teachers will forget to close a window when everyone leaves school at the end of their day. (Which, by the way, is not even close to sundown, so I don't know why they call it the end of the day. People get confused so easily!) Even if the window is open only a crack, I can get through because I am very fluffy. I am able to squeeze and wriggle my way in to visit my cousins and my honorary cousins.

Science

At the end of the school day, after all the big yellow buses that take the people children away from school leave, and after all those people children who walk or ride bikes leave, and after all the teachers leave, I jump from branch to branch in the schoolyard and check the windows. One teacher has not closed one of the windows tight. This is the room where my cousins the geckos live.

I pause to think: Does my head feel clear enough to take on my cousins?

No wibble-wobbles at all, so I will risk it.

I suck in my stomach, scrunch down my fur, and wriggle through the opening the teacher has left for me—either by forgetting or by wanting me to come in and share my knowledge with the geckos.

The geckos start talking even before I get halfway in.

One says, "I'm Galileo," at the same time the other one says, "I'm Newton."

They introduce themselves every single time I come into their room, so maybe they can't remember that they've told me this before. Or maybe they don't remember who *I* am. Or maybe they don't trust my memory—or my ability to tell one of them from the other. I admit this takes concentration, seeing as they have no fur, just like newborn squirrel babies.

I say, "Hi, cousins."

They start talking in the way that I know will eventually give my head the wibble-wobbles.

GALILEO: We're not actually cousins, you know.
NEWTON: We're geckos, and you're—
GALILEO: —a squirrel.
TWITCH: Well, yes, but—
NEWTON: That means we're reptiles.
GALILEO: While you're a mammal. Not the same thing at all.

NEWTON: Not at all.

TWITCH: I—

GALILEO: Our scientific name—

NEWTON: —is *Phelsuma Gekkonidae*.

GALILEO: And you're from the genus—

NEWTON: *Sciurus*.

TWITCH: By *cousins,* I meant—

GALILEO: The closest we are to being family members is that we're both members of the animal kingdom—

NEWTON: —as opposed to being in the plant or fungi kingdom.

GALILEO: Which is such an obvious observation, it's silly.

NEWTON: It's not nice to call a fellow scientist silly.

TWITCH: He didn't—

GALILEO: I didn't call you silly, I called your observation silly.

NEWTON: You always think you know better.

GALILEO: That's because I'm the older brother.

NEWTON: No, *I'm* the older brother. I was born first.

GALILEO: Mother laid the egg with you in it first, but I hatched first. That makes me older.

TWITCH: Speaking of brothers, I have—
NEWTON: Me.
GALILEO: Me!
NEWTON: ME!
TWITCH: Why don't we change the subject?

GALILEO: I'm named after Galileo Galilei.
NEWTON: I'm named after Sir Isaac Newton.
TWITCH: I'm named after—
GALILEO: Galileo Galilei was born before Isaac
          Newton, just the way I was born before
          my brother Newton.
NEWTON: *Yes* to the scientist Galileo being born
          first. *No* to the gecko Galileo being
          born first.
GALILEO: And everybody likes Galileo better. He has
          a museum named after him: the Galileo
          Museum and Science Center. The children are
          taking a field trip there tomorrow.

TWITCH: What's a field trip?

NEWTON: A field trip is when the children take an educational trip away from the school.

GALILEO: But they don't go to a field.

NEWTON: Except in October, when the kindergarten children go to a pumpkin field—

GALILEO: Patch. Pumpkins grow in a pumpkin patch, not a pumpkin field. Silly younger brother.

NEWTON: A pumpkin patch is just another name for a pumpkin field. *You're* the silly younger brother.

GALILEO: Anyway, this is not October. And the children who use the science lab are not kindergarten children.

NEWTON: I didn't say they were.

GALILEO: So I don't even know why you brought it up.

NEWTON: To explain about field trips.

TWITCH: Thank you.

GALILEO: The science museum sounds like a wondrous place.

NEWTON: Wondrous.

GALILEO: Sort of like a science fair . . .

NEWTON: But without anyone trying to demonstrate how to make a stink bomb.

GALILEO: Or how to shoot potatoes out of a potato cannon.

NEWTON: Or how to tame a feral cat and make it into a pet.

TWITCH: Nobody ever tries to make a squirrel into a pet, do they?

GALILEO: We wish we could go to the science museum. The children get on a special bus and are gone for most of the day.

NEWTON: When they return, they are full of stories of all the scientific marvels they have seen.

TWITCH: Can't you go to the science museum with the children?

GALILEO: Oh, no.

NEWTON: Definitely not.

GALILEO: We need our heat lamp.

NEWTON: We need the safety of our vivarium.

GALILEO: Outside, there are snakes.

NEWTON: And hawks.

TWITCH: And owls. Still . . .

GALILEO: To go on a field trip, we would need to sneak onto the bus and not be seen.

NEWTON: Then get off the bus at the museum and not be seen.

GALILEO: Then get back on the bus and *still* not be seen.

NEWTON: To return to school.

GALILEO: To the science lab.

NEWTON: To our vivarium.

GALILEO: We wish we could go, but we cannot.

NEWTON: We cannot.

GALILEO: Definitely not.

NEWTON: Even though the science museum—

GALILEO: —the Galileo Museum and Science Center—

NEWTON: —is the place to go to have all your scientific questions answered.

Finally the geckos have run out of words and stop talking.

I'm remembering the wolves my mother has warned me about, but which nobody in my family has ever seen.

I tell the geckos, "I have scientific questions I want answered!"

Traveling the
Scientific Way

The next morning I sit in a tree and watch as the yellow school buses leave one after the other.

And, because I'm such a good thinker, I think: Why are the buses called *yellow*? They are definitely not the color of daffodils or dandelions or forsythia blossoms or any other yellow flowers I can think of. The closest I can come to that color is marigolds, which can be yellow or orange, and if you look at a patch of them all together and squint your eyes, that's the color of school buses. So why aren't buses called *something-sort-of-but-not-exactly-like-marigolds?*

My honorary cousins the geckos like to be accurate about everything they say—they tell me that's the scientific way. I resolve to be more scientific, too. From now on, I will call buses *something-sort-of-but-not-exactly-like-marigolds-colored,* and I will encourage others to be accurate that way also.

I'm so busy thinking these deep thoughts, I almost don't notice that all of the buses except for one have left. The geckos told me that this was what would happen, and that the one remaining bus would be the field trip bus. The children have gone from all of their various buses into the school to be counted, and soon they will come out and board this one bus to ride to the museum and science center that's named after my cousin the gecko.

One thing that both my gecko cousins agreed on is that I must not be seen getting on the bus, even though I explained to them that everybody loves squirrels, and that I would be welcomed. But they told me that— loved or not—nobody is allowed on the buses besides the driver and the children. A special exception is made for field trips, when select parents and teachers will be named as chaperones. Chaperones are those in charge of keeping the children from wandering off and getting lost, since people children do not stick close to the nest, the way well-behaved squirrel children do.

I will trust that the geckos are right when they say I should not let myself get seen.

They also advised against simply climbing to the top of the bus and riding there. They talked about crosswinds and wind blasts and wind shears and wind gusts, not to mention lift and drag and aerodynamics, until my head was ready to wibble-wobble right off my shoulders.

"No riding on top," I promised them.

So now I'm watching the bus driver, who is sitting in his seat and has the bus door open. He's reading a book and probably would not notice me going up the same stairs the children do, because people tend to not notice quite a bit of what goes on around them.

But several of the windows are open, so I decide it's just as easy to go in that way.

I jump from the branch that's closest to the bus (I'm an excellent jumper) and land on the roof of the bus (I'm an excellent lander). From here I can see into the window of the room in the school where the geckos live. I stand up and wave at them. They must think I have not listened to their advice and plan to ride here, because

I see one of them lift his little foot with  its tiny padded toes—not to wave back, but to clap against his forehead.

So that they won't worry, I don't linger but go to the edge of the roof of the bus. Holding on to the edge, I swing down and in through the open window.

I land on one of the seats.

The bus has many seats, and they all face toward the front. That's the same arrangement as in the classrooms in the school, except that in the classrooms, the teacher faces the children, and on the bus, the driver faces away from them. I stand on the seat where I've landed and look where everyone will be facing. It is just another window. If they want to see outside, they should go outside, where they'd have a clearer view.

The driver puts down his book, but not because he's seen me. He's seen the children who are to go on the field trip, who are bursting out of the front door of the school. The geckos were certainly right that the children seem excited about their field trip. They are talking and laughing and running—even though the teacher chaperones call out, "Walk!"

One of the children is neither running nor walking. He is riding in a metal chair with two big wheels in back and two small wheels in front. I have seen this child before. Sometimes he turns the big wheels with his hands to make his chair roll; other times one of the teachers pushes his chair to make it go. I have heard other children offer to push the chair, but the teacher always says no because they will push it too fast. I have seen the boy go pretty fast on his own.

The driver and the teacher work to get the chair onto the bus, which gives me a little time, but not enough to explore the bus or to search out the perfect hiding place. So I simply jump down to the floor and hide under one of the seats.

Stomp! Stomp! Stomp! The children's feet make the floor shake, but I know nobody can step on me where I am.

Oops! I realize maybe I'm not as safe as I thought as a boy throws himself into the seat where I *was* and swings his feet to where I *am*. I dodge, moving closer to the wall of the bus.

"The sooner you find seats, the sooner we can get going," the adult people tell the people children.

It would be hard for the children *not* to find seats, since the bus is made up almost entirely of seats.

Still laughing and talking and stomping, the children find seats.

There's a loud noise as the bus starts. I've heard buses start before, but it sounds louder from the inside.

And the children sound even louder than they do on the playground at recess.

Probably the geckos have a scientific reason for this to be so.

Then the bus moves, and I unexpectedly find myself sliding backward. I look up and I'm no longer seeing the bottom of the seat under which I was hiding. I'm seeing the boy with the big feet. Luckily, he's too busy poking the boy next to him and neither one of them sees me.

I scramble back to *under* the seat ahead of the two boys and dig my nails into the floor.

But every time the bus stops or starts or turns a corner, I have to fight to hold on. Having to hold on is like when I play on the squirrel playgrounds people put in their yards around the food they set out for us. There are slides and swings and sometimes it's a real challenge to get to the actual squirrel feeder with its yummy snacks.

I wonder if this is what the geckos meant by aerodynamics.

Speaking of snacks, something besides me that is sliding around on the floor is half a peanut butter sandwich. I wonder if one of the children has seen me and is sharing, or if the sandwich got left behind by accident. People can be careless with their food that way. In any case, offered or forgotten, I munch the sandwich, between sliding and holding on.

Finally the bus stops. I have been concentrating on not sliding backward or to the sides, but this time I slide forward. I slide between a pair of pink sparkly sneakers and the only thing that stops me from sliding forward even more is a pink sparkly bag—the kind people call a backpack.

I scramble back before the girl who owns the pink sparkly sneakers and backpack can see me.

The driver calls out to everyone, "It looks like rain, so close the windows. I'll be parked here. Here is where you come back to at two fifteen. Have a good time."

Yikes! If the windows are closed, how will I get off the bus without being seen? I don't want to have come all this way just to wait on the bus while all the children get to see the Galileo Museum and Science Center.

And the most bothersome thing of all is: the bus driver is wrong. One good sniff of the air, and I can tell that it's not going to rain until evening. That bus driver's nose doesn't work properly.

I look at the pink sparkly backpack that stopped my slide. I can tell by the way the pink sparkly sneakers are planted firmly on the floor facing sideways that the girl who is wearing them is busy closing the bus window nearest her.

The backpack has a buckle and a zipper. The girl hasn't buckled the buckle or zipped the zipper. There's no time to search out a better choice, so I dive into the backpack.

There's a notebook and some pencils and an apple in here. An apple! How thoughtful of the girl! I always have room in my tummy for an apple. I think better of the girl even though her backpack is decorated with a picture of a kitten wearing a pink sparkly dress, which makes me very nervous. I hope the girl doesn't think it's a good idea to put a squirrel into a sparkly dress.

But before I can have second thoughts, I feel the girl lift the backpack and start walking.

One of the teachers claps her hands in that way that means *Please be quiet and listen.* "Children," she says, "I know you will be on your best behavior anyway, but I wanted to warn you that the museum was considering canceling all the field trips today because they have been having trouble with thefts. Please be aware that— because of this problem—they will be inspecting all backpacks and bags before we leave."

If *inspecting* means what I think it means, I'll have to find a different way to leave the museum than the way I am getting in.

But meanwhile we are leaving the *sort-of-but-not-exactly-like-marigolds-colored* bus and going into the museum and science center.

All I can do is start munching that apple.

Dinosaurs

I bounce in the backpack as the girl bounces into the museum. I have noticed that people children bounce a lot more than the adult people. Squirrels bounce when they walk, too. I wonder if that means we're related. I'll have to ask the geckos.

The temperature changes as the girl goes from the bus (hot and stuffy) to outside (warm and pleasant, due to the sun being out—pay attention, Mister Bus Driver!—no rain coming) to inside the museum (chilly).

In fact, the children start saying, "Cool!" But

they're saying it in such an excited and pleased-sounding way that—after several of them add the word "Dinosaurs!"—I remember people sometimes use the word *cool* to indicate they like something.

I also know the word *dinosaurs*. On the playground, sometimes children talk about dinosaurs or read books that tell about them. I have climbed to a branch above where the children sit when they choose to sit quietly rather than running and climbing and sliding, and I have looked down at the pictures in those books.

Dinosaurs are animals.

Except they are make-believe animals.

I know this because I've never seen a dinosaur, and other squirrels I've asked have never heard of them. This makes them different from the wolves, which we haven't seen in as long as any of us can remember but which squirrel mothers still warn about and which I am going to be learning all about at the museum today.

Squirrels don't make up animals. We have enough to worry about with owls and weasels and foxes.

But sometimes the people teachers read books to the children about make-believe creatures. Besides dinosaurs, these include dragons and unicorns and kittens that sparkle.

In fact, dinosaurs and dragons are clearly related

to each other—and not just honorary cousins like me
and the geckos. The difference is that in the stories,
dragons talk and fly and breathe fire and have all sorts
of exciting adventures. Dinosaurs pretty much just eat
each other.

So when I hear the children squealing, "Dinosaurs!"
I assume that the museum is like a library and has
books with lots of pictures. I make my way to the top
of the backpack and lift up the flap so that I can see
and—if a story is to be read—hear.

There's nothing to see in the direction I'm facing, so I squiggle around to look in the same direction the girl is looking. I have trouble making sense of what I'm seeing.

It's not books. It's not a picture.

It's very, very big. Even by people-sized standards.

One of the children cries out, "T-Rex! My favorite!"

I recognize the name. "T-Rex" is the most famous dinosaur, just as "Bambi" is the most famous deer, and "Charlotte" is the most famous spider, and "Scooby-Doo" is the most famous dog, and "Winnie" is the most famous pooh. (Which is another made-up animal.)

Although, clearly, I have to stop thinking of T-Rex as being make-believe.

I've seen pictures of T-Rex, and I realize that's who is standing before me. (Well, actually, he's standing before the little girl with the pink backpack. I'm behind her, peeking over her shoulder.)

The little girl must be a fan of the adventures of T-Rex, for she steps closer, even though he has a reputation for being very fierce. If she's going to engage in risky behavior, maybe it's time for me to leave the backpack. Although T-Rex isn't moving at the moment, he's looking right at us with glassy eyes, and his jaws are enormous and filled with pointy teeth. I suspect he could swallow both of us in one bite.

But before I have a chance to scramble entirely out of the backpack, the girl moves even closer. If she thinks that little velvet rope that's surrounding the area he's in is going to protect her, she hasn't listened to the same stories I have. "Look!" she yells, even though all the other children are already clustered around, already looking. "There's his bones, and there's the model!"

I don't know what a model is. But: bones! That's what's left after something gets eaten. I've seen bones before, but not standing upright on their own. Has T-Rex eaten something so quickly that the bones haven't had a chance to fall down yet? What's the matter with the teachers, bringing children to such a dangerous place? And what's the matter with those two geckos, talking me into coming here?

Incredibly, one of the adults who must work at the museum is standing *inside* T-Rex's enclosure. Maybe the little girl is assuming T-Rex will eat him first, and that will give her and the other children time to escape.

But the museum worker doesn't seem worried. He smiles and tells the children, "Welcome to the Galileo Museum and Science Center. I trust you'll have a fun and informative few hours here. But meanwhile,

I see you've noticed our newest exhibit. The bones are actual fossils, dug up in Alberta, Canada, then carefully reassembled here by our knowledgeable on-staff paleontologists. Then our ingenious lab people made the full-sized model of what he might have looked like when he was alive. He may be plastic, but doesn't he look real?"

Plastic is what people make toys out of. I have seen plastic T-Rexes before, but those were small enough to fit into a child's pocket. I breathe a sigh of relief. T-Rex *is* make-believe. I should have trusted my nose. There is no scent of a living creature here besides the people—and me, of course.

"And," the museum worker says, "just to make your experience more memorable, our animatronic specialists have added voice and movement."

This museum worker uses words that are too big. The teachers would know better. He will lose the interest of the children, who can become bored very easily.

But before there is a chance of that, he pushes a button and T-Rex roars, swinging his massive head and snapping his jaws.

The children shriek. Even the adults gasp.

I am not afraid. Squirrels are very brave. But squirrels

are also very smart. It is not smart to stand in front of something that is roaring at you. I scramble out of the backpack and onto the head of the girl in pink so that I can leap to safety.

The girl—who had *not* been one of the ones to scream at a dinosaur roaring at her—now screams at having a squirrel on her head. She also starts bouncing in place. This makes me bounce, too, which makes it hard for me to get my footing for my jump.

Even if squirrels ate little girls—which they do not—I could not swallow her in a single bite the way a dinosaur could. So I don't understand why she is more frightened of me than of the dinosaur.

Meanwhile, the other children are not paying attention to the screaming girl. Their shrieks have turned to laughter. "Again!" they cry at the museum worker. "Make him do it again!"

This is because T-Rex is not a living creature. He is a very big, very noisy toy.

I'd forgotten that for a moment.

The only one who hasn't stopped screaming is the little girl whose head I'm sitting on. She's flapping her arms in the air, not swatting at me, but like a chicken trying to take off.

People finally notice that she's still screaming,

still bouncing. They turn to her. They point. They say, "What's that on your head?"

"I don't know!" she screams.

Well, this explains why she's upset. Since I climbed up the back of her head, she must not realize that I'm a squirrel. Still, I'm amazed at the lack of education shown by the other students, who can't recognize what I am—unless they can't see because of all her hair, or because of all her bouncing.

Even though people can't understand Squirrel (though squirrels can understand People), I lean close and make the chittering sound in her ear that means *squirrel*. Even if she doesn't know the meaning of the word, she should be able to recognize what kind of animal is speaking.

The girl is not reassured. "Get it off! *Get it off! GET IT OFF!*"

Climbing out of her backpack and onto her head probably was not my wisest decision.

"It's a squirrel!" someone shouts. "Stop making such a fuss!"

I look over and see the boy in the movable chair.

He calls over to the girl, "He's probably more scared of you than you are of him."

I'm not scared at all. I was only startled, for a moment, by the dinosaur's roar.

The girl doesn't believe him, either, and she doesn't stop screaming.

Some of the teacher chaperones are heading in my— our—direction in that fast walk teachers often use at the same time they're saying, *"Now you're in trouble."*

So I leap off the girl's head and run.

The Gift Shop

I run through a forest of legs. Most of them are moving away from the girl whose backpack I was riding in. Sure, gather around the dinosaur, scatter away from the squirrel!

But this unreasonable behavior of people works out well for me because all the movement makes it hard for the adults to keep track of me. I know that people love squirrels, and there's always the danger of someone wanting to keep me as a pet. Squirrels are not meant to be pets.

The first room I come to is no bigger than a classroom at school, but there are no desks for sitting at or boards for writing on or clear aisles for walking down. It is crowded wall-to-wall with people stuff: on shelves, hanging from the ceiling, on counters. If there is something in here to teach about wolves, I will never find it. Still, this will make a good place to hide for a while. The shelves hold brightly colored boxes of all shapes and sizes. There are also some of the plastic T-Rex toys I have seen children playing with on the playground—pocket-sized, which I think is a very sensible size for T-Rex to be. There are other toys of the kind that are soft. There are whirly things hanging from the ceiling, twisting and catching the light. There are books. There are barrels and bins and baskets. There are butterfly nets, which I recognize from spring in the schoolyard. There are . . .

Oooo! Candy bars! I've tasted little bits of candy bar that the children sometimes accidentally drop during recess. Chocolate is delicious, and I haven't eaten in forever. Well, except for the apple that was in the backpack. And the peanut butter sandwich on the floor of the bus. And the French fries I found in the garbage can at the edge of the playground before I got onto the bus. Not to mention my breakfast of seeds and nuts. And my snack of green tomatoes that someone thoughtfully planted for me, with a fence to keep deer and chipmunks and groundhogs out.

But other than that, my tummy is entirely empty.

How kind of these people to welcome me to the science museum by leaving a whole bunch of candy bars out for me!

What's the best way to get onto the counter?

I jump onto a shelf and stretch to reach up to the next higher shelf.

Someone screams, "A rat!"

Rats are my cousins! I look around to find this cousin. But I don't see him.

I look at the person who screamed. She's dressed like the other museum workers, and she's pointing at me. I turn around just to make sure. But no. She's definitely pointing at me. I wag my tail at her: my big, fluffy squirrel tail, which is entirely different from a rat's skinny, naked tail.

But apparently she's not interested in being educated, for she keeps screaming, "A rat! A rat! There's a rat in the gift shop! Somebody get a security guard!"

I have to pause to consider. Everybody loves squirrels, so I know that means they would want me to have the candy bars. But I'm not sure they feel the same way about rats. So . . . as a squirrel who is being mistaken for a rat, should I still make myself at home with the candy, or not?

Truth is truth, I decide. I should take one of the candy bars. Sooner or later, someone will tell her, "No, that was a squirrel you saw, not a rat," and then she would feel bad if I *didn't* take one. I don't want her to feel bad, even if she can't tell the difference between a rat and a squirrel.

I climb the rest of the way onto the counter and reach into the jar where the sized-for-squirrels candy bars are. These have easy-to-remove wrappers, which is good because when I pop one into my mouth I taste mint, which is not my favorite. I spit it back out into the jar for somebody else and choose another that turns out to be chocolate and almonds. Yummy! My favorite!

A new museum person runs into the room. I wonder if he's the security guard help that the woman called for. I know what a *crossing* guard is, but there are no people children needing to cross a street here, so I don't know what a security guard's job could be. This man is tall and skinny and has just shiny skin on top of his head, but the rest of his hair is long and tied back into a ponytail. He takes one look at me, then grabs one of the butterfly nets.

Clearly, he's one of those people who would want to make a pet out of me, so it's time to leave.

I leap from the counter to a tall stack of boxes.

Security Guard tries to sweep me up into his net, but he knocks the top box off the pile because I've already jumped onto this tall thing that has slots for holding and showing shiny pictures. Surprisingly, the thing begins to spin around. And tip.

The woman who can't tell the difference between a squirrel and a rat yells at the man, "Careful! Those telescopes are delicate! And now he's on the postcard rack!"

I don't know what a postcard rack is, but at least she's not yelling "Rat!" anymore.

Security Guard picks up the box he caused to fall and gently shakes it. He checks out the woman and sees she isn't watching him, so he hurriedly sticks it back on top of the pile.

Meanwhile, the woman lunges to grab hold of the tall, slotty, spinny thing I'm riding on, no doubt worried that I might get hurt if it falls.

But there's no cause for alarm, as I've already jumped onto one of the things hanging from the ceiling. This one looks like a bird—if birds were wooden. The string holding it breaks, and I fall—unhurt because squirrels know how to fall safely—and I land on a soft pile of T-shirts.

Too bad for Security Guard, though. The wooden bird lands on his head and he jumps, causing the box he just replaced—plus two others—to crash to the floor.

And too bad for the woman, too. Because the place is so crowded, when she reaches to catch the tall, slotty, spinny thing, she knocks over a container that is on the counter. The container is full of those small, really bouncy balls that the children sometimes play with on the playground.

The container *was* full of those balls. Now they spill, they hit the ground, they bounce, they go off in all directions.

The woman steps back from the bouncy balls and knocks into a display that has little baskets full of sparkly stones. They fall, too. But they don't bounce.

She hasn't learned to stop moving. She takes another step, putting her foot on one of the stones, and loses

her balance. She throws her arms out to keep from falling and sweeps a bowl of marbles onto the floor. She ends up falling into the arms of Security Guard, who catches her but knocks over a stand that holds pens and pencils and crayons and markers.

What a mess they've made!

I run out of the room before someone starts yelling at them.

The Hall of the Planets

The next doorway leads to a room whose walls curve around in a circle. (I know my shapes from listening in at the school window of the first grade.) I recognize people from the field trip bus, but I don't see the girl whose backpack I rode in.

Is she still by the dinosaur, screaming? I wonder. I listen but she must have stopped, for squirrels have excellent ears, and I'd be able to hear her, even from this other room.

This room is as dark as outside right after sunset.

Those children and adults who are in here with me are moving slowly and looking upward. These two things are good because they mean nobody will be noticing me on the floor so no one will be trying to claim me as a pet. I just need to avoid their feet.

I dart left.

I dart right.

I dart around.

I dart between.

Once in a while, my tail brushes someone's ankle, and they squeal, "What was that?"

But by the time they look, I have darted somewhere else.

But all that looking up they're doing makes me curious, so I look up, too, to see what's so interesting, just in case it's something good, like fruits or nuts about to drop from above, or something bad, like an owl circling hungrily.

What I see are balls of various sizes and colors hanging from the ceiling.

The reason it's so dark in here, especially near the floor, is because the only light comes from the biggest ball, which is glowing as it hangs there in the center. It is also the only one sitting still while the others move around it. The children reach up, stretching, but the balls are too high above for them to be able to touch.

The people at the museum may have planned this.

Even though there clearly is nothing about wolves here, I decide the dark makes it safe for me to stay for a little while to listen and learn—which is what the geckos told me to do. But I keep on darting: left, and right, and around, and between.

"So these are the planets," a girl says, "which means that one must be the sun. So, is that the earth?" Her face is tipped upward to see the planets rather than forward to see where she's going as she walks to keep up with a blue-and-green ball overhead. It's about the size of an apple.

Teachers like to answer questions with questions, so I guess it is a teacher who answers, "Is it the third one from the sun?"

Another probably-teacher asks, "Is two-thirds of it covered by blue for water?"

From behind me, just coming in, is a voice I recognize as the voice of the boy with the movable chair. Maybe he hopes to be a teacher someday, for he too answers with a question: "Does it have a sign on the wall saying it's the earth?"

The girl who asked leans against the handrail that goes along the entire circle of the wall. There are signs here and there on the wall, with little lights over them, and the girl peers at one of them. "Oh, they included the moon, too," she says, but then she looks up to check.

I look up, too. There is what looks like a giant gray blueberry near the blue-and-green apple planet.

The boy in the chair says, "This isn't right."

I know what he means. We live on the earth. Obviously the earth isn't round, or we'd fall off. The moon *is* round—except when it isn't—but it's not a blueberry.

The boy says, "This isn't accurate. It isn't to scale."

The only scales I know are on snakes, so I don't know what he's talking about.

Neither does the teacher who is pushing the boy's chair. "What do you mean?" the teacher asks.

The boy says, "The solar system is too immense to be shown to scale in any room. It would take more than three million earths to fill the sun. This sun, here, is about the size of a beach ball. That means the ball representing the earth should be just a little bit bigger than a pea, and Mercury would be the size of the head of a pin."

"That would be hard to see," one of the other children acknowledges. The planets stop moving, and he pushes a button on the wall, which gets them going around the room once more. "But if that's the right way, that's the way they should show it."

I think so, too. The geckos said science is about facts.

The boy in the chair shakes his head, which—for people—means *no* even though for squirrels it means *something's gotten into my ear.* The boy says, "But then the room would have to be about a mile and a half long."

"Know-it-all," someone says, in a tone that indicates that knowing all there is to know is a bad thing—even though it sounds like a good thing to me.

Someone else asks one of the teachers, "Is that true?"

The teacher says, "Ahmmm. Well. Ahhh. Don't forget, I teach math, not science."

"It is," says the girl who is still by the sign on the wall that tells which planet is which. "It says so here, on this sign, under *Facts.* It says this display is to show the order the planets are in, and which are big ones and which are smaller ones. Ooo, and it says if you include Pluto, Pluto would be the size of a dot made by an extra-fine pen, and that it would be two miles away."

"I don't think they should have gotten rid of Pluto," another child says.

Squirrels don't have planets, but when most of the children call out their support for Pluto still being a planet, I agree with them because it isn't nice to not include everyone.

They teach that—along with shapes—in first grade.

More children start to crowd around the girl to look at the *Facts* sign by her, even though there are plenty of other *Facts* signs around the room, and I get nervous that they are so intent on reading facts that one of them will step on me. Other people have come into the room, and nobody is leaving. There are just too many feet blocking my way to the door I came in, and there are even more feet between me and the second door, which leads farther into the museum—to where I will learn about wolves.

I dart left, right, around, between—and I'm no closer to a door than I was before.

So I climb up onto one of the big wheels of the boy's movable chair.

Neither the boy nor the teacher notices me. But then the teacher says, "Well, why don't we move on to the next exhibit and make room for others to see this? I hear they have pieces of meteorites and lunar rocks and a Mars rover model." And with that he starts pushing the chair.

I'm holding on to the side of the wheel, not the rim, so I don't get run over, but I go around once . . . twice . . . three times . . . and I'm getting dizzy.

When the spot where I'm holding on once more reaches its highest, I jump off the wheel and onto the boy's lap, hoping he won't notice.

But he does. He gives a squeal just as loud—but not as long—as the backpack girl did when I first climbed onto her head.

I jump from his lap to the handrail that keeps the children from actually touching the *Facts* signs. From there I jump onto one of the planets that's overhead. Luckily, the one that happens to be closest to me is the biggest, so it's easy to catch hold of even though it takes an expert jumper like me to make it.

The ball begins to swing back and forth even while it continues to move in a slow, steady trek around the room and the glowing ball in the center.

All of a sudden, nobody is interested in whether Pluto should still be a planet.

There's a lot of gasping and squealing, and then people start shouting:

"It's a squirrel!"

"It's that squirrel that was on Lydia's head!"

"It's gotten onto Jupiter!"

The planets are moving at different rates of speed, but only Jupiter is swinging.

I jump onto another planet, and this one has a ledge around it, which makes my hold even steadier even though now *it's* swinging, too.

Except that there's a loud *crack!* and suddenly the ledge is tipping downward.

"There go the rings of Saturn!" someone shouts.

Some of the children duck and cover their heads and scramble to the edge of the room as though afraid I'll lose my grip and fall on them. At the same time, others crowd in for a closer look.

"Let me through! I've got a net!" calls a voice I recognize as belonging to Security Guard.

A net doesn't sound good.

But the boy in the movable chair cheers me on: "Squirrels in Space! You go, squirrel!"

My Saturn-ball is about as far away from the center of the room as its journey around the sun takes it, so I jump again before the ledge can break off entirely. Good thing I jump when I do: Saturn's ledge breaks free of Saturn, Saturn breaks free of the string holding it,

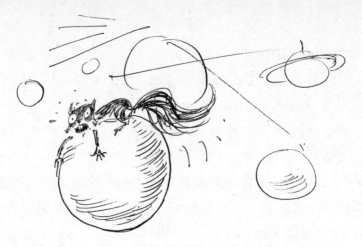

and both pieces hit Security Guard on his shiny head, one after the other.

"Ow! Ow!" he says.

The new ball I'm on is much smaller, but it's the one that's farthest away from the light in the center that's meant to be the sun.

"Neptune!" the children sing out the way they do on oral quiz day.

Because Neptune is so small compared to the last two planets I was on—it's a bright blue grapefruit—I need to curl myself around it, and its swinging is enough to make even a surefooted squirrel eager to move on. I see I'm approaching the door that leads farther into the museum.

And—since I've learned all there is to know about planets—I jump.

Mars Rover

I jump off Neptune in one room and onto a table made out of glass in the next. It's like a window, except it's going the same direction as the ground instead of reaching up and down like the windows at school. But it's definitely a window on this table because I can see through it. Still, there isn't a schoolroom on the other side. It's more like a big box. But the box isn't holding anything interesting. Just a bunch of stones.

I jump to the next table. When I look through *that* window, I see somebody's clothes. The clothes are all puffy, like what the children wear when they go outside to play in the snow, since they don't have fur to keep them warm the way squirrels do. But this set of clothes is big, like for a grown-up, not a child.

There are also very thick gloves, and boots, and something round that comes with its own small, curved window attached. In the table box, there is a list of facts, like there was on the wall in the room with the planets.

The facts include a picture of a man wearing these clothes, and he has the round thing on his head. Even though it goes all around his head, this reminds me of the helmets worn by the children who ride their bicycles to school. I have heard the teachers who wait outside say, "Put on your helmet to protect your head in case you fall." The grown-up who wears *this* helmet must not be very good at all at riding his bicycle if he needs so much more protection than the children do.

I hear the sound of footsteps running into the room, and I decide there is no time to look at any more of the tables.

In this room there is another, smaller room made entirely of windows—the regular up-and-down, side-to-side kind, not the lying-flat kind. The windows of this room within a room go all the way down to the floor, but they don't go all the way up to the ceiling. It's just like the fish tank in the third grade. But people-sized.

And without the fish.

Or the plants that sway in the water.

Or the water.

Or the little treasure chest that opens and closes, opens and closes.

I jump from the window table to on top of one of the fish-tank-room windows. From here I see that Security Guard has run in. He has a second Security Guard with him. This one has curly hair on his head, and his big belly jiggles as he runs. He is carrying a blue plastic box like the ones at school, where the teachers say *Bottles and cans in the blue bin, papers in the yellow bin*. If there were bottles and cans in *this* blue bin, Bin Guy has lost them from holding the bin upside down.

I also notice that there were children in here all along. They aren't looking at the window tables. (No wonder! They're boring!) Instead, the children are looking into the window room. I have noticed what's not in here (fish, plants, water, treasure chest), but now I look to see what *is* here.

I see something very like a sandbox. I know sand-boxes from the school playground and a few of the yards nearby.

Inside this sandbox, someone has built up hills and dips and scattered stones like the ones in the first table box. There is also something else. It is about the size of the backpack I rode in, but I don't know what it is.

The teacher said this room holds a Mars rover model. I don't know what that is, either, so I wonder if the two things I don't know are the same thing.

I balance on the top edge of the window. The museum worker called the dinosaur in the first room a model, so I wait to hear if the Mars rover model will roar, too.

"There he is!" the teacher who pushes the boy's movable chair shouts at the two security guards. "By the Mars rover exhibit! Get him before he jumps in!"

Why would I jump in?

There must be something interesting that I can't see from on top.

I decide that jumping in sounds like a fine idea.

The sand in the sandbox is more dirt than sand. Also, there are no toys. A good sandbox has pails and shovels. Here there are only the stones and Mars Rover. Sometimes in the school sandbox there are treats which the smaller children have brought with them during recess but which have fallen into the sand, and then the children don't want them anymore.

I don't know why.

I look for treats, but there aren't any of those, either. It's been *so long* since I've eaten.

I sniff at Mars Rover, wondering if that's something to eat, but it's not. Just metal.

Suddenly Mars Rover moves, jerking forward on its wheels as though startled by my sniffing it. I jump, too, startled by Mars Rover being startled. I put my paw out to touch, to make certain Mars Rover isn't a live thing.

No, it feels like metal, just the same as it smells like metal.

Mars Rover moves forward a bit more.

I notice that there are children crowded around the fish-tank-room windows, watching.

One girl is sitting at a chair that is up against one of the windows. She is wearing great big glasses and great big gloves. Some of the children are crowded around *her.* "Move it again!" they tell her.

She does something with her hand, and Mars Rover moves again.

"I don't want to scare him," she says. "But it's my turn to use the virtual reality controls. I've been waiting for, like, forever."

"Turn it so the camera's facing him," someone tells her.

Again she twists her hand. This time Mars Rover doesn't move forward, but a metal tube swings around until it's pointing at me.

The children around the girl cheer, but I don't know why. I sniff at the tube that moved and is now facing me. The children are laughing and excited when I press my nose against the glass at the end of the tube, but I still don't know why. I climb up onto Mars Rover for a better look.

Security Guard tries to get the girl to move away from the big gloves and glasses so he can sit in the chair, but she says she waited her turn, and it would be unfair of anybody to make her move so soon after she got there, and she doesn't want to start yelling unless she has to.

She moves her hands again, and Mars Rover very slowly begins to roll forward on its wheels. This reminds me of riding on the field trip bus, except bouncier so that I have to hold on to Mars Rover the whole time, and not just when we start and stop and turn corners.

And this time I'm not hiding under a seat, so I can look around. Mars Rover rolls up and down over some of the hills in this sandbox. Once in a while it moves another metal piece that scoops up some of the dirt or one of the stones, sort of like a shovel.

"Just keep him moving," I hear Bin Guy tell the girl. I see that Mars Rover and I are headed toward the back window of this fish-tank room. Security Guard has come to this side. He has opened a glass door and is standing there—which would be good, since that will be an easy way out. But it's not good, because Security Guard is holding a net.

Does he think I can't see him?

I will have to move quickly.

Moving quickly is a squirrel specialty.

Mars Rover is bringing me closer and closer to the door. I'm almost there. Security Guard has the net raised. In one more moment I will jump off Mars Rover and zig and zag past man and net.

With the teacher watching Security Guard, the boy with the movable chair makes his chair bump right into where the girl with the gloves is sitting.

She jerks her hands, and Mars Rover runs over Security Guard's foot, just as though the foot was another hill.

Security Guard yelps in surprise.

Bin Guy comes running and slams the upside-down blue plastic bin over Mars Rover—and onto Security Guard's foot.

But not over me. I have already jumped off. I run past both of them and into another room.

Science Stuff

The next room *still* doesn't have anything about wolves. What it has is a big circle in the middle of the floor. (These museum people really seem to be fond of circles.) Like the room with the planets, there's a ball hanging from the ceiling. But the cord that holds it must be broken, because this planet is swinging back and forth very close to the floor.

There is a museum worker here, and he is talking to the children who are gathered around the circle. But he does not say, *The planet in this room is broken.* He says, "This is a Foucault pendulum. If you look up, high above your heads, you can see where the pendulum is attached to the dome three stories up. Down here, the pendulum swings back and forth. But—because the earth rotates on its axis—each swing of the pendulum brings it closer to one of the bowling pins placed on the floor at precise intervals as on a clock face. Every ten minutes—accurate to the second by careful scientific calculation—the pendulum will knock over one pin. If you don't mind waiting, or if you want to come back, the next pin will be knocked over in seven minutes and thirty-six seconds on the dot."

Blah, blah, blah. Too many big words!

Boring!

Besides, I hear Security Guard's big feet. I hear Security Guard's big voice: "Stop that squirrel!"

Yet another security guard has joined Security Guard and Bin Guy. Like Security Guard, this new person has a ponytail, but while his is gray, hers is brown.

Security Guard still has his butterfly net, Bin Guy still has his blue plastic bin, and Ponytail is carrying a puffy coat.

Ponytail's voice is just as loud as Security Guard's when she shouts, "Don't let that squirrel near the pendulum!"

It's not that I want to get near that broken pendulum planet, but—with all those children gathered around the big circle on the floor—near the broken pendulum planet is the only spot not blocked by feet.

I run. I jump. I land on the planet called Foucault Pendulum. I shinny up the metal cord that attaches the planet to the ceiling until I am higher than the heads of the children and the adults. The cord swings and sways and twists and twirls.

The museum worker was wrong about the children having to wait for this planet to knock over a pin. It knocks one over right away.

The children cheer, "The squirrel scores!"

Security Guard swings his net just as Bin Guy tries to scoop me up with the blue bin. The broken planet swings into a second pin and then a third.

Ponytail tosses her coat at me but misses, and more pins fall.

The children cheer, "The security guards score!"

Three is as high as I can count anyway, and I leap off the cord.

My skillful jump takes me beyond the circle of children gathered around the Foucault Pendulum planet. Many of the children in this different part of the same room have turned to see what is going on with all the shouting around the broken planet. But a few continue what they were doing, which is watching one of the other children, who is standing on a platform with her hand touching a metal ball about the size of a young groundhog. This is the same girl with the pink sparkly backpack. There's a teacher with this group of children, and he says, "Notice how the Van de Graaff generator makes static electricity that causes Lydia's hair to stand on end."

My jump—have I mentioned I'm an excellent jumper?—has landed me on the girl's poufy head. I feel my fur ripple up and away from my body in a tickly way.

I hear one of the other children call out, "Notice how Lydia has a squirrel on her head!"

Even if I hadn't recognized the girl before, I would recognize her by her scream.

I look around for someplace else to jump. Nearby is another ball—this one is baby-groundhog-sized. It is clear, and it has lightning inside it. A boy is heading straight toward it saying, "I want to touch the plasma ball."

There's a museum worker here who does not warn, *Stay away! Lightning hurts!* Instead, he lets the boy place one hand on the ball, then gives him a glass stick to hold with the other hand. The glass stick begins to glow.

Over the sound of the pink sparkle girl screaming, I hear the museum worker say, "My! It's noisy in here today!" Then he asks, "Does it hurt?"

I think he should have worried about that before he let the child touch the ball.

But the boy tells his classmates, "No," and the museum worker says, "I told you it wouldn't. Anybody else want to touch the plasma ball and light up the bulb?"

I do not, even though the lightning does not seem able to get out.

Instead, I jump onto a table that has balls of different sizes floating over it—they're not attached to strings, just floating. The table has air blowing out of it, which startles me. (Not *frightens—startles*.) I back away from the breezy spot on the table.

And right into another gust of air.

I move sideways and into another strong blast of wind. And then another. As I move, each of the balls stops floating, one after another. *Drop! Drop! Drop!*

Security guards 1, 2, and 3 have picked up their net, blue bin, and coat. "By the Bernoulli air pressure table!" Security Guard shouts, pointing at me. They have seen me, but they don't see the balls on the floor. The security guards drop, too. *Drop! Drop! Drop!*

"Somebody get that squirrel!" Security Guard shouts from the floor.

The three security guards have gotten their arms and legs tangled, so they are having trouble standing back up.

I jump off the drafty table and onto the floor. Across from me, a set of doors open, sliding into the wall. I run into the room, but it is very small. It is also filled with a group of children and one teacher. They all back against the walls when they see me. None of them scream, but a few do squeal. I'm guessing they're happy squeals—since everybody loves squirrels.

Since there is nowhere to go from here, I'm about to run out the way I came in, but the doors slide back, closing us all in together.

One of the children says, "Hit the button for the second floor," and one of the others pokes at a button on the wall just as the teacher says, "No, hit *open doors*."

The doors do not open. The floor shakes a bit, and I feel that the room is moving—like the school bus. I watch the children, to make sure none of them is planning to capture me and make me into a pet.

"Don't make eye contact," one of the children whispers to the others.

"It's a squirrel," the teacher whispers back, "not a crazed ninja hypnotist."

But he doesn't look into my eyes, either.

And I'm not looking at the teacher. I'm looking at one of the children, who is holding a bag of potato chips. I'm just thinking how very, very hungry I am when he lets the bag fall to the floor. The room isn't moving *that* much, so I know he must have dropped it on purpose.

I leap forward and grab one of the chips. It's the polite thing to do, since he offered them.

Usually the potato chips in the garbage can by the playground are small and soggy, but this is big and crispy and oh-so-yummy.

Then the doors slide open, and the room *is* like the school bus, because we've moved to a different place.

"Floor two," says a voice that comes from the ceiling, an adult woman's voice even though there are only children, one man teacher, and one squirrel present. "Natural history diorama displays."

I hold one more potato chip between my teeth, then run out of the small room.

"Stay on," their teacher tells me—or maybe he means the children. I can't stay. I have scientific questions that need to be answered. None of the children from the movable room follow. They just let the doors close again. They must be more interested in moving than in getting someplace.

Dioramas

I am in a long hallway that has big windows on each side. These must be the natural history diorama displays, whatever that means.

There are more children here, and they're running back and forth, back and forth, back and forth, and not using their indoor voices. I also hear the same adult voice that I heard in the movable room. But a whole lot of people must have the same voice, because I hear her saying a whole bunch of different things all at the same time so that I can't even make out the words.

Every time one voice goes quiet, one of the children runs up to the buttons that are by each window and slaps it, and the voice starts again. The children are so busy running and making the voices talk they don't even notice me.

I finish eating my potato chip, then run to one window and look in.

On the other side of the window is a room smaller than the classrooms at school. In this room there's the top part of a tree, even though I don't see the bottom part. I can see sky behind the tree, but I can't smell anything—probably because of the glass.

Now that I'm standing right in front of this room, I can hear the voice that goes with it. The voice is saying, ". . . their summers in the Arctic Circle, but they visit our part of the Northern Hemisphere in the winter. You are most likely to spot a snowy owl by the shoreline or in agricultural fields . . ."

Yikes! And in science museums! After noticing all those other things first, now I see that sitting on one of the branches is an owl! Owls eat squirrels! His wings are spread and I know that in a moment he will fling himself off the branch and into the air. Yes, there's glass between us, but I haven't had a chance to look closely.

This might be like the fish-tank room with Mars Rover in it that had no top.

There's no time to look now.

I run.

I zig and zag among the children. The floor is slippery so that my feet move faster than my body and I go sliding and skidding around corners and into children.

These children didn't see me before, but they see me now. Especially when I accidentally run into them. Some of them scream. I take this to mean that the owl is close.

There are many hallways branching away from the one I first saw. Each hallway is lined with more little glassed-in rooms that are diorama displays, with the voices talking.

There is no place to hide under.

A door opens, and security guards 1, 2, and 3 come through carrying their net, bin, and coat. I see stairs behind them, but the door closes before I get there.

Security Guard points at me and says, "There he is!"

I have never before met a person who is so determined to make me into a pet.

I think to myself, *Better to be a pet than to be dinner.*

But still I run into a group of children, so that their

legs will hide me—from security guards and from the owl.

Ponytail throws her coat and captures one of the children.

Over the children's squeals, I hear Bin Guy ask, "Where?"

And Security Guard answers, "By the snowy owl diorama."

Double yikes! Somehow I have gotten twisted around and ended exactly back where I started.

And the owl is right there, fierce and ready to swoop and grab me up in his talons!

But . . .

That means he couldn't have been chasing me.

Why is he exactly where he was before, in exactly the same eager-to-snack-on-Twitch pose?

I realize this owl is another model, a toy like T-Rex. Now I can see that even the sky isn't real but is just a picture. What's the matter with these museum people, having dinosaurs and lightning balls and owls where they can scare children?

The doors to the movable room open, and there are even more children in there than before, including the boy in the movable chair, but this time they are coming out. Should I run there?

The door to the stairs opens, but a whole bunch of children are coming that way, talking and laughing excitedly. Should I run there?

And another door opens, but there's only one person standing in that doorway.

I decide that's where I need to run.

"What's going on here?" the museum worker who is standing alone asks. "What's all the noise? Quiet, everybody! Children!" She claps her hands. "Indoor voices!"

She's so busy trying to get the children quiet, she doesn't even notice me running past her into the new room. And when Security Guard shouts, "He's going in the staff lounge!" she only puts her finger to her lips and repeats, "Indoor voices."

No diorama displays in here. And no people.

This room has lockers, like in the hallways at school, but not as many, and tables, like in the cafeteria at school, but not so many of those, either.

What there's lots of is places to hide under.

But there's also food on one of the tables. It's been so incredibly long since I've eaten! I climb on the table, but by then I'm going so fast, I crash into somebody's plate and glass, and then—zoom!—slide right off the other end.

Luckily the dish comes along with me, so I don't have to climb back up the table. The dish had lots of veggies in it: lettuce and tomatoes and broccoli and radishes. And there's cheese, too, and slices of hard-boiled egg, which is something people invented that makes my stomach sing with happiness. Without that egg, it would have been hard to choose. I cram some egg into my mouth, then run and hide under a bookcase.

I wonder if there are books about wolves in there.

I wonder if there are books about squirrels.

Probably, because people love squirrels.

People come running into the room: the museum worker who wanted the children to be quiet, the children (who have not gotten quiet), the teachers who were with the children, and security guards 1, 2, and 3—all pressing into the room.

"He's got to be here somewhere," Security Guard says, swinging his net in the air as though he thinks squirrels can fly. He accidentally hits Bin Guy on the head, making him drop his blue bin, which lands on Security Guard's foot. Ponytail is looking for someplace to fling her coat.

People start shouting suggestions about where they think I might be hiding.

"Find him!"

"Check behind that couch!"

"Check inside that couch!"

"Move that coatrack!"

The boy in the movable chair is not shouting suggestions.

Maybe because his chair makes him closer to the

ground than anybody else, he tips his head and looks under things.

He sees me under the bookcase. I will have to leave my hiding spot before I've even finished chewing my egg.

Except . . .

He does not tell anybody. He puts his finger to his lips in the same way the museum worker did to signal *Quiet.*

Of course I can be quiet. Squirrels are good at being quiet when they need to be.

Staff Lounge

There are security guards, children, teachers, and museum workers crowded into the staff lounge room— all searching for me. Most of the people are running around, looking behind things, looking under things, looking on top of things, looking behind/under/on top of things they've already looked behind/under/on top of. Those who aren't running around are shouting advice about where to look.

"Look in the cabinet under the sink."

"Did you move the cushions on the chair?"

"What about behind the refrigerator?"

"What about in the refrigerator?"

All that activity makes me want to run back and forth, too.

Especially when I see that the person who picked the spilled food off the floor didn't notice one of those small tomatoes. Nobody else notices, either.

My empty tummy tells me how very good that tomato would taste. I imagine my teeth pressing into the firm skin, then the sudden *pop!* and the squirt of juice in my mouth. Mmmm! It's not very far from where I'm hiding under the bookcase.

But then someone's foot kicks it away. And somebody else's foot kicks it in a different direction, still *away*. It bounces off the table leg and goes spinning toward one of the chairs. But yet another foot kicks it before it rolls underneath, and now it's within a quick dash-and-grab of me.

The boy in the movable chair sees me watching the tomato and he raises a hand the way the crossing guards at school do to signal *Stop*.

Someone else kicks the tomato and now it's farther from me than before. I'd better go for it before it gets too far away.

But then, before I move, I hear Security Guard ask,

"Did anyone look under the bookcase?"

Uh-oh!

I back up, but there isn't far to go. The sides and back of the bookcase go all the way down to the floor, so there's no way out but through the front—where I can see the feet of Security Guard coming toward me.

The boy in the movable chair wheels himself between me and Security Guard and asks, "What about the lockers? Shouldn't you search those?"

Security Guard stops walking toward me. "How would he get in?" he asks. "They're all closed."

"But they don't have locks," the boy says. "He might have. You don't *know* he didn't. Squirrels have hands, and that's one smart squirrel."

I am, I think. I'm a very smart squirrel.

Security Guard growls, "That's one dead squirrel if I get my hands on him. I plan to wring his neck."

Oooo, so not a pet after all. I wonder if he could be a wolf.

A little girl starts crying. *She'd* want me as a pet.

The museum worker who was in here eating all that glorious food tells Security Guard, "That's no way to talk." She tells the little girl, the children, everybody, "Don't worry. I'm the director of the museum, and what I say goes. We will capture the squirrel live and release it unharmed outside."

If I get to choose, that definitely sounds better than neck-wringing.

The museum worker-director says to Security Guard, "Why don't you check the lockers?"

Grumbling, he turns away from the bookcase. He opens a locker, slams it shut, opens another locker, slams it shut . . . The boy in the movable chair looks at me and pats next to himself, the seat of the chair.

I think he's trying to help, but I'm not sure.

Everybody else is facing the lockers.

I decide now is the time to catch that traveling tomato.

I dart out from under the bookcase, and—oops!— it turns out not everyone is watching Security Guard open and close lockers. "There he is!" calls out the girl who was crying before. Then she adds, "You meant that about not hurting him, didn't you?"

A little late to check now!

I run to hide back under the bookcase, but everybody's watching, so that's no good. I change direction as quickly as that tomato bouncing off someone's toe. I go under the table. Too open. The food that spilled has made the floor slippery, and I skid when I try to change directions. I slide away from the chair close to the door and find myself near the couch instead. I climb up onto the couch and run along the back.

"Run, squirrel, run!" calls out the boy in the movable chair.

Security Guard is closer than I thought. He swings his net—just as one of his big feet lands on my beautiful tomato, squishing it. His leg slips sideways in all that juicy juice, and I fling myself off the couch and at the row of lockers behind.

The lockers turn out to be metal (I never knew that!), and that means nothing for my nails to dig into. There are slits near the top that would make a great place to hold on, but between them and me is smooth slippery metal. Despite my scratching and scraping, I slide down the face of the locker until I get to the handle, which stops my slide. I manage to get my back feet and my front feet onto the handle, and I can jump onto the counter once I have my footing.

But before I can jump, there's a *click!* and the locker door swings open. Wheee! I twist around to the other side of the door—the side that's usually inside—and leap into the locker and catch hold of a coat that's hanging from a hook (not the coat Ponytail has been

throwing at me and children). I climb up the coat and onto a little shelf that's in the locker. It's crowded on the shelf because there's a plastic bag like some of the students carry their lunches in to keep their food cold. I sniff the bag, but I don't smell food.

From this higher spot, I can jump up and across to the top of the thing they called refrigerator. Then I can climb down the back of that, run behind the chair that's close to the door, and run out of this staff lounge.

The only thing stopping me is that bag, which takes up too much room. I can make a better jump if I start from a level spot. So I push the bag off the shelf. It hits the floor with a thud.

Then there's a second thud.

Which is Security Guard slamming the locker door shut with me trapped inside.

Caught!

I expect to hear Security Guard say, *I've caught you now!*

But what I hear instead is Museum Director Woman. "*What,*" she demands, "is that?" She uses the same tone teachers use when they know exactly what the *that* which they're asking about is. They're not really looking for an answer—they're just letting the children know how much trouble they're in.

Bin Guy says, "Those look like some of the moon rocks that have been going missing the last few days."

From my shelf, I can see out the slits in the top part of the locker door. Children and teachers and museum workers are gathered around the floor where the bag I pushed—the one for holding lunches—has landed. The top has opened, and two stones the size of strawberries have rolled out. They are like the stones I saw in the glass table in the room with Mars Rover. Stones are not as interesting as strawberries. I wish I had a strawberry now. Strawberries are my favorite thing.

"Whose locker is this?" Museum Director Woman asks.

Bin Guy and Ponytail look at Security Guard.

"It's my locker," he says, "but I never saw this bag before."

"I've seen you carry your lunch in it every day this week," Bin Guy says.

"So have I," says Ponytail.

"So have I," says Museum Director Woman.

"I mean," Security Guard says, "yes, obviously, it's my bag, but I have no idea how the rocks got in

there. I've never seen *them* before. Except in their case, naturally. Which I never opened."

"It's you," Museum Director Woman says. "It's you who's been stealing the rocks, and you've been sneaking them out of the museum in your lunch bag."

The little girl who pointed me out asks the question I've been wondering. "Why would he steal rocks?"

The boy in the movable chair says, "They're from the moon."

Museum Director Woman says, "Which makes them very hard to get. And *that* makes them very valuable. Even the small ones we have."

"Boo! Hiss!" the girl says to Security Guard.

"You can say that again," says the boy in the movable chair.

"Boo! Hiss!" the girl repeats. "You're in so much trouble."

That will teach him to chase a squirrel.

And to make such a mess in the museum.

"We'll call the police from my office," says Museum Director Woman. She takes the butterfly net from Security Guard's hand.

Bin Guy has put down his blue plastic bin, and Ponytail puts down her puffy coat. They each hold on to one of Security Guard's arms.

Everybody is watching them.

Except for the boy in the movable chair. He rolls his chair closer to the locker, and he opens the locker door a crack. Once again he pats the seat.

I slide down the coat that is hanging from the hook. Then I climb up onto the chair next to the boy. He arranges his backpack beside him so that it forms a roof over me. I can see out, but people can't see me. He leans down and peels the squished tomato off the floor and hands it to me. Most of the juice is gone, but it's still delicious. That's why tomatoes are my favorite.

The museum people have left the room, and the teacher who has been pushing the movable chair says, "Well! That was exciting. But now we'd better rejoin the rest of the class."

The movable chair is a much smoother ride than either the school bus or Mars Rover. In the hallways with the diorama displays, a new group of children is running back and forth pushing the buttons that make the voices explain what's inside.

"The sea otter's coat is water-repellent to keep this aquatic creature warm and dry . . ."

"The buffalo was hunted to near extinction in the 1800s . . ."

"The bald eagle is the only eagle unique to North America, which is why . . ."

"Timber wolves are social animals that live in family units called packs . . ."

Wolves!

I put my head up, and the boy stops the chair.

There are two wolves in the diorama display we are facing. Like the owl that startled me earlier, the wolves are not moving, but they look as if they could lunge in an instant. They are bigger than foxes or weasels, but not as big as T-Rex. But they have almost as many teeth. I remind myself that even if the wolves are real (and they probably aren't), they are behind glass. They can't smell me any more than I can smell them. From my hiding spot between the arm of the chair and the backpack, I show my teeth to the wolves. I tell them, "Boo! Hiss! You're not that scary."

As long as they stay behind the glass.

But—just in case—I will definitely continue to tell young squirrels, "Don't let a wolf eat you."

Life Lessons

It's not that I've become the pet of the boy in the movable chair. It's just that we ride in his chair together.

He has a bag of peanuts in his backpack, and he shares them with me. Anytime one of the museum workers talks for too long or uses words that are too big, the boy reaches into the bag. One peanut for him, one peanut on the seat beside him for me. He even cracks the shells open for me. That's the sign of a true friend. Did I mention peanuts are my favorite thing?

I stay next to him even when the field trip is drawing to a close and the teacher and the bus driver get the chair back into the field trip bus.

Of course, it has *not* rained (because I know weather better than the bus driver does), so the bus is warm and stuffy. While the children and the teachers open their windows, I climb down from the chair, but I stay under the seat in front of the boy where he can see me and I can see him.

And where I am still in range of thrown peanuts.

Once again, I have to hold on every time the bus starts, stops, or turns a corner.

The ride back to school is even noisier than the ride to the museum. Children are talking and laughing

and singing songs, and the teachers are too tired to tell them to use their indoor voices. The children have all gotten cookies and candies from the gift shop and share with one another. The teachers all hide in the back of the bus.

When we reach school, the other children start getting off the bus first.

One of the children, who has not zipped her zippers or buckled her buckles, has picked up her pink sparkly backpack the wrong way, and suddenly everything that was in her backpack is now on the floor of the bus. The children who are still on the bus are helping her to gather up all the spilled notebooks and pencils and hair fasteners—all of which are also pink and sparkly. The children are blocking the way and I decide I've waited long enough.

"Thank you for the peanuts," I tell the boy, even though I know he can't understand me. But it's always a good thing to be polite, no matter what.

I jump onto the seat in front of me, climb up to the back, and see that beyond the girl with the pink sparkly backpack, the way is clear.

I spring from the back of the seat, touch down for just the tiniest moment on the girl's head, then leap off and run down the aisle of the bus. A quick bound down the stairs, and I'm outside—where squirrels belong. Up a tree I go.

Behind me, I can still hear the screams of the excitable girl, even though I'm gone.

The boy in the movable chair is saying, "Lydia! It was just a squirrel. And he's gone now." Then he says, "Goodbye, squirrel!"

I can't be sure, but I think he sounds sad.

I'm a bit sad, too.

After all of the children get on their regular buses to go home, I find the window to the room where my cousins the geckos live. The window is once again open a crack, and I squeeze in.

"I'm Galileo," says one.

"I'm Newton," says the other.

"I'm Twitch," I say. "I'm just back from the museum."

GALILEO: That would be the Galileo Museum and Science Center.

NEWTON: We know the name of the museum already. You don't have to remind anybody.

GALILEO: He could have meant the art museum, which is named after some artist person.

NEWTON: But he wasn't going to the art museum. He was going to the science museum.

GALILEO: Which is named after me.

NEWTON: Which is named after the man you're named after.

GALILEO: Same thing.

NEWTON: No, it's not.

GALILEO: Yes, it is.

TWITCH: I had a good time.

NEWTON: Did you see marvels of science?

GALILEO: Did you see demonstrations and exhibits?

NEWTON: Were there untold wonders to behold?

GALILEO: Did you gain scientific wisdom?

TWITCH: I learned some new life lessons.

For once the geckos stop talking before my head has started to wibble-wobble. They want to hear what I have learned.

This is what I tell them:

- School buses are not really yellow. They're *something-sort-of-but-not-exactly-like-marigolds-colored.*
- A pocket-sized dinosaur is better than a big dinosaur.
- Planets can break and fall down easily.
- Mars Rover is a fine sandbox toy.
- Sometimes lightning can get in a ball, and if it does, then it's not dangerous.
- Wolves are not as scary as a security guard with a net.
- Peanuts that a friend has cracked open for you are absolutely the best thing in the world. The only things that are better than peanuts a friend has cracked open for you are hard-boiled eggs. The only things that are better than hard-boiled eggs are squirrel-sized chocolate bars. The only things better than squirrel-sized chocolate bars are potato chips. The only things better than potato chips are peanuts that a friend has cracked open for you.

For another once, the geckos *still* do not have anything to say. I can see that I have shared scientific wisdom with them that they did not know before.

"Oh," I say, "and one more thing: I learned Sir Isaac Newton's real name."

The two geckos look at each other, then they look at me, then they look at each other, then they look at me.

NEWTON: Sir Isaac Newton's real name *is* Sir Isaac Newton.
GALILEO: Definitely his real name.
NEWTON: I've never heard of another.
TWITCH: It's Fig. And guess what. He has a cookie named after him. I tasted one on the bus. It's the best—

GALILEO: No, I don't think—
NEWTON: Ha! Having a cookie named after you is better than having a museum named after you.
GALILEO: No, it's not.
NEWTON: Yes, it is.

GALILEO: A museum is big and important.

NEWTON: A cookie is something children love, so obviously they love Newton better than they love Galileo.

GALILEO: Do not.

NEWTON: Do too.

GALILEO: Not, not, not.

NEWTON: You're just saying anything in order to have the last word.

GALILEO: Not.

I leave my cousins to work this out for themselves.

All this talk of cookies has made me hungry. Science is fine, but I need to get my dinner. I plan to look for a cookie. Cookies are my favorite thing.

Galileo and Newton: A Brief Explanation of Everything

GALILEO: The thing about Twitch is that sometimes he gets so excited it's hard to tell what he's talking about.

NEWTON: This doesn't mean we don't like him.

GALILEO: Of course not. We like him a lot.

NEWTON: Even if he thinks we're cousins.

GALILEO: When we're not.

NEWTON: Definitely not. But sometimes his understanding of science is not exactly what one could call . . .

GALILEO: Correct.

NEWTON: I was going to say *complete*. That's a little less judgmental.

GALILEO: And a lot less accurate. So let's talk about the science of his field trip, starting with—

NEWTON: —the bus. School buses are school-bus yellow. It will never catch on to call them *something-sort-of-but-not-exactly-like-marigolds*.

GALILEO: What to call the color of school buses is not a scientific question.

NEWTON: Which we have now firmly settled. That brings us to—

GALILEO: —the dinosaurs. Since the last of the dinosaurs died out long before people came on the scene, we have to deduce what they looked like by the clues—mainly their bones that fossilized after they died.

NEWTON: Some museums display actual dinosaur bones.

GALILEO: Some museums display casts or replicas because the bones can be fragile or rare.

NEWTON: And some museums display models showing what the dinosaurs *might* have looked like with skin, but this is guesswork. For example, scientists who had never seen a gecko but were trying to put together a picture of us from just our bones might give us scales in a pink-and-purple checkerboard pattern.

GALILEO: But probably not.

NEWTON: They might.

GALILEO: I don't think so.

NEWTON: Let's move on to—

GALILEO: Planets. Twitch was absolutely right that there has never been a picture or a model of the solar system that is accurate.

NEWTON: That's because the distances are so vast.

GALILEO: There's a lot of space in outer space.

NEWTON: I just said that.

GALILEO: I said it better.

NEWTON: That's why we need scientific instruments like the Mars rover to help us explore places that are too far away for people to get to safely.

GALILEO: Actually, there have been several Mars rovers. The first one was built in 1996.

NEWTON: And it took seven months to get from Earth to Mars.

GALILEO: It's a one-way trip. The rovers pick up

samples to analyze and send the resulting data—

NEWTON: —and pictures—

GALILEO: —to the scientists back on Earth who control the Mars rover by computer. Moving on, the Foucault pendulum was invented by Jean-Bernard-Léon Foucault more than 150 years ago to prove that the earth rotates.

NEWTON: A pendulum on a clock swings back and forth, back and forth quickly because the pendulum is short.

GALILEO: Even the pendulum on a grandfather clock is short, compared to a Foucault pendulum, which hangs at least three stories above the floor.

NEWTON: So a Foucault pendulum swings slowly. Back and forth, back and forth.

GALILEO: But meanwhile, the earth is rotating, which is what causes day and night. And the earth's movement makes the Foucault pendulum *look like* it is not only going back and forth—

NEWTON: —back and forth—

GALILEO: — but also moving in its swinging path in a circular pattern.

NEWTON: When all the while, it's the earth that is moving—even though we can't feel it.

GALILEO: And the only direction the pendulum has actually moved is back and forth.

NEWTON: Back and forth. I like to say it twice to indicate the continued motion.

GALILEO: Of course you do. Next comes the Van de Graaff generator, which has a rubber belt—

NEWTON: —like at the checkout in a supermarket—

GALILEO: —that goes around and around two rollers made of different materials. Next to each roller is an electrode.

NEWTON: The electrodes are metal pins that collect the charge from the belts—

GALILEO: —and pass it along to the hollow metal ball on top.

NEWTON: The electrical charge—

GALILEO: —passes harmlessly through anyone touching the ball but makes the person's hair stand on end.

NEWTON: Geckos don't have any hair.

GALILEO: It's the same idea as when you shuffle your feet on a rug, then touch somebody else and give off a shock of static electricity.

NEWTON: But, again, not so much with geckos.

GALILEO: The plasma globe, or plasma light, was invented by Nikola Tesla in the late 1800s. It's a glass sphere filled with gases—

NEWTON: —such as neon—

GALILEO: —and also has an electrode in the center. The electrode charges the neon, and that creates energy. You see that energy as strings of colorful light. Different gases create different colors.

NEWTON: Like with the Van de Graaff generator, it's safe to touch, so long as you're standing on something that isn't metal. When Twitch saw the student light up the fluorescent lightbulb, that was because the electricity passed from the plasma ball, through the student and the lightbulb, then out through the museum worker and into the ground.

GALILEO: Another thing you can do is make the electricity in the plasma ball move by touching the outside of the ball with your finger.

NEWTON: Geckos don't have fingers. We have digits.

GALILEO: Some geckos don't have much of a brain.

NEWTON: That's not a nice thing to say to your brother.

GALILEO: I didn't say *you*. I said *some*.

NEWTON: It was clear what you meant.

GALILEO: You're too sensitive. Let's move on to the Bernoulli air pressure table. Daniel Bernoulli lived in the 1700s, but his observations about air pressure helped people develop airplanes—

NEWTON: Many, many years later.

GALILEO: Yes, Newton, many, many years later. On the Bernoulli air pressure table, air is forced out of nozzles tilted in different directions. Where air is moving faster, there is less pressure.

NEWTON: That means you can place things like Ping-Pong balls or golf balls or beach balls in the stream of air, and they'll float.

GALILEO: And they stay floating even if the nozzle is tilted to the side—

NEWTON: —unless there's a squirrel running across the table.

GALILEO: Yes, as long as the stream of air is not disturbed, the blowing air has lower pressure than the surrounding air, and—

straight up and down, or off to the side— the object placed in that area of lower pressure defies gravity and rises.

NEWTON: With an airplane, there's no Bernoulli air pressure table. It's the shape of the wings that causes air to flow faster over the wing than under, which causes lower pressure above than below, which causes lift.

GALILEO: I already said that.

NEWTON: You didn't say that Sir Isaac Newton helped develop this principle.

GALILEO: No, I didn't mention that.

NEWTON: Which is why people named the Fig Newton cookie after him.

GALILEO: The Fig Newton cookie was not named after Sir Isaac Newton.

NEWTON: Well, it wasn't named after Galileo Galilei.

GALILEO: It's not important.

NEWTON: It is to the people who eat the cookie.

GALILEO: All right, then.

NEWTON: You don't always have to have the last word.

GALILEO: Fine. You can have the last word this time.

NEWTON: Good. So that is the true story behind what Twitch saw at the science museum.

GALILEO: The Galileo Museum and Science Center.

NEWTON: You said I could have the last word.

GALILEO: So long as you're accurate.

NEWTON: So that is the true story behind what Twitch saw at the Galileo Museum and Science Center.

GALILEO: The end.

Read more books about Twitch and his adventures!

"A whole lot of fun."
—*Kirkus Reviews*

Nominated for seven
child-voted state awards

"This is a story young
readers will love."
—*School Library Journal*